Harry Houdini

To Addison, held fast in her Oma and Opa's hearts forever
and for always — E.M.

 ® Kids Can Read is a registered trademark of Kids Can Press Ltd.

Text © 2009 Elizabeth MacLeod
Illustrations © 2009 John Mantha

Kids Can Press acknowledges the financial support of the Government of
Ontario, through the Ontario Media Development Corporation's Ontario Book
Initiative; the Ontario Arts Council; the Canada Council for the Arts; and the
Government of Canada, through the BPIDP, for our publishing activity.

Published in Canada by   Published in the U.S. by
Kids Can Press Ltd.   Kids Can Press Ltd.
29 Birch Avenue   2250 Military Road
Toronto, ON M4V 1E2   Tonawanda, NY 14150

www.kidscanpress.com

Edited by David MacDonald
Designed by Marie Bartholomew
Printed and bound in Singapore

Educational consultant: Maureen Skinner Weiner, United Synagogue Day School,
Willowdale, Ontario.

The hardcover edition of this book is smyth sewn casebound.
The paperback edition of this book is limp sewn with a drawn-on cover.

CM 09 0 9 8 7 6 5 4 3 2 1
CM PA 09 0 9 8 7 6 5 4 3 2 1

Library and Archives Canada Cataloguing in Publication

MacLeod, Elizabeth
    Harry Houdini / written by Elizabeth MacLeod ;
illustrated by John Mantha.

(Kids Can read)
ISBN 978-1-55453-298-8 (bound).
ISBN 978-1-55453-299-5 (pbk.)

1. Houdini, Harry, 1874–1926 — Juvenile literature. 2. Magicians — United
States — Biography — Juvenile literature. 3. Escape artists — United States —
Biography — Juvenile literature. I. Mantha, John II. Title. III. Series: Kids Can
read (Toronto, Ont.)

GV1545.H8M32 2009   j793.8092   C2008-907084-4

Kids Can Press is a *l'orus*™ Entertainment company

Harry Houdini

Written by Elizabeth MacLeod
Illustrated by John Mantha

Kids Can Press

Who could make an elephant disappear?
  Who walked through brick walls?
  Who wriggled out of handcuffs,
even underwater?
  Who could escape from any lock
and chain?

Who was one of the most amazing
magicians ever?

Harry Houdini, that's who!

Harry Houdini's real name was Erik Weisz (VISE). His family and friends called him Ehrie (AIR-ee).

Ehrie was born in 1874, in a country called Hungary.

Ehrie

Ehrie's father could not find a job. So when Ehrie was two, his father traveled by ship to the United States. He left behind his wife and five sons.

In the United States, Ehrie's father lived in Wisconsin. He worked hard and saved his money. Two years later, he had saved enough to bring over his family.

When Ehrie was eight years old, he saw his first magic show. The magician Ehrie watched was named Dr. Lynn.

In his magic act, Dr. Lynn seemed to cut off a man's arms, legs and head. After that, Dr. Lynn magically put the man back together again. Ehrie clapped wildly.

Acrobats also amazed Ehrie. He loved watching them swing from trapezes.

Ehrie got his own trapeze and worked on tricks. Kids in the neighborhood paid to see Ehrie perform. He called himself the Prince of the Air.

By 1883, Ehrie had a sister and another brother. Once again, their father had trouble finding work. The family was very poor.

One snowy day, Ehrie was begging on the sidewalk. He stood perfectly still, holding out his cap. As snow piled up on his head, coins piled up in his cap.

Ehrie hid the money in his clothes.
Then he raced home and told his mother
to shake him. Coins flew everywhere!
It was Ehrie's first magic trick.

But Ehrie got tired of always being cold
and hungry. When he was 12, he ran away
from home.

In New York City, Ehrie got a job. But he did not forget how much he loved magic.

When Ehrie was 17, he and a friend created a magic act. Now they needed a name for themselves that people would remember.

Ehrie decided they should use Houdini as their last name. He chose for himself the first name Harry. It sounded like his nickname, Ehrie.

Harry and his friend called their act
The Brothers Houdini.

With his friend, Harry performed many card tricks. The two magicians also made scarves appear out of candle flames.

Harry made a flower appear in a buttonhole on his suit. He even made a scarf magically change color.

Later, Harry performed with different partners. Then, in the spring of 1894, Harry met Bess Rahner.

Bess was a singer and dancer. She and Harry fell in love and got married. Soon Bess became Harry's partner on stage.

Harry and Bess's best trick started with Harry stepping into a cloth bag. The bag was tied tightly shut. Then it was locked in a trunk.

The trunk was tied with thick ropes. Then it was then rolled into place behind an open curtain.

Bess clapped her hands three times. As she quickly pulled the curtain closed, she stepped behind it. Instantly the curtain was pulled open — by Harry!

Where was Bess? She was sealed in the bag inside the locked trunk!

People loved Harry and Bess's trick. But audiences were bored by the rest of the show. Soon few people were coming to see the Houdinis.

By 1899, Harry sadly decided he must give up magic forever. But he and Bess still had a few shows they had to perform.

A man who hired acts for big theatres saw one of their shows. He loved Harry and Bess's escape trick.

"Forget about the small magic tricks," the man told the Houdinis. "Just perform escapes."

Harry and Bess decided to try it.

Soon Harry and Bess became a huge success. But Harry knew his audiences might quickly get bored again. So he invented new tricks.

In 1907, thousands of people gathered on a bridge to watch Harry be wrapped in chains and handcuffed.

Harry took a deep breath and jumped into the river below. Would he drown?

Suddenly Harry burst up out of the water. He had escaped the chains! In one hand, he held the unlocked handcuffs.

The crowd loved it.

The next year Harry performed his Milk Can Escape. First, he was handcuffed. Then he squeezed into a milk can.

The can was filled with water, and the lid was locked shut. Harry had to escape — or drown.

Seconds ticked by. The audience went wild when Harry finally appeared.

In 1912, Harry added a new trick to his act. He hung upside down in a glass case full of water. Heavy clamps held his feet.

But in minutes, Harry escaped!

Before long, Harry had another escape trick. Out on a sidewalk, he was strapped into a special jacket. The jacket trapped his arms tightly against his body. It seemed impossible to escape.

Next, Harry was lifted high into the air. He dangled upside down far above the crowd below.

Harry wiggled and twisted. Soon he had wriggled out of the jacket. Harry had escaped again!

By now Harry was one of the most famous people in the world. Crowds gathered wherever he went. Newspapers wrote stories about his amazing escapes.

Harry was also rich. He earned much more money in a week than most people earned in a whole year.

In October 1926, Harry was performing his magic tricks across the United States and Canada.

While he was in Montreal, Quebec, Harry talked with some college students in his dressing room.

One young man asked Harry if it was true that Harry could be punched in the stomach and not be hurt.

"Yes," said Harry. "But first I need to get ready."

Before Harry was ready, the student began punching him. Harry finally made the young man stop.

Harry's stomach was incredibly sore. He barely made it through his show that night.

Later that night, Harry took the train to his next show in Detroit, Michigan. He was in a lot of pain. But he decided to give one more show.

When the show ended, Harry was rushed to the hospital. It was too late. Harry died on Halloween.

People still talk about Harry's incredible escapes. He used his skill and his imagination to perform tricks that had never been seen before.

Who is the most famous magician of all time? Harry Houdini — that's who!

More facts about Harry

- Harry was born on March 24, 1874. He died on October 31, 1926.
- All of Harry's tricks were very dangerous. Never try to do one of these tricks yourself.
- Harry starred in six movies. You can still watch some of them on DVD.
- Dogs were Harry and Bess's favorite pets. Harry even trained one to escape from tiny handcuffs.